Hippity Skippity EASTER

by Maria Fleming 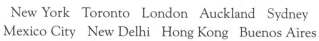 Illustrated by Katy Bratun

SCHOLASTIC INC. Cartwheel BOOKS®

New York   Toronto   London   Auckland   Sydney
Mexico City   New Delhi   Hong Kong   Buenos Aires

For Mom and Dad,
with love
—M.F.

For Ania, Eric, and Jill
—K.B.

ISBN 0-439-56417-4

Text copyright © 2004 by Maria Fleming. Illustrations copyright © 2004 by Katy Bratun. All rights reserved. Published by Scholastic Inc. SCHOLASTIC, CARTWHEEL BOOKS, and associated logos are trademarks and/or registered trademarks of Scholastic Inc.

Library of Congress Cataloging-in-Publication Data

Fleming, Maria.
Hippity skippity Easter / by Maria Fleming ; illustrated by Katy Bratun.
p. cm.
"Cartwheel books."
Summary: While delivering eggs to his animal friends, Easter Bunny has an accident and his friends must find a way to cheer him up.
ISBN 0-439-56417-4 (pbk.)
[1. Easter~Fiction. 2. Rabbits~Fiction. 3. Animals~Fiction. 4. Easter eggs~Fiction. 5. Stories in rhyme.] I. Bratun, Katy, ill. II. Title.
PZ8.3.F6385Hi 2004
[E]~dc21
2003005396

10 9 8 7 6 5 4 3 2 1   04 05 06 07 08

Printed in the U.S.A.   23
First printing, February 2004

Hippity, hop.
Hippity, hop.
Easter's here,
no time to stop.

Hippity, skippity,

down the road,
with eggs for Chipmunk,
Bee, and Toad.

One for Ladybug.

One for Mouse.

 One for Owl in his green tree house.

Hippity **HIGH.**

TO CHIPMUNK'S HOUSE

Hippity LOW.

Hippity, zippity.

GO! GO! GO!

Uh-oh . . .watch out, Bunny!

STOP!

STOP!

STOP!

Hippity,

trippity,

flippity

FLOP!

Eggs go flying through the air.
Shatter, scatter everywhere.

So sad, Bunny.
Boo-hoo, hoo.

Not one egg is left for you.

Sniffle, snuffle, shuffle home.
Sit and cry, all alone.

Friends come racing—
hurry, scurry.
They can fix it.
Do not worry.

A little tape. A little glue.

Ta-da! HOORAY!

Good as new.

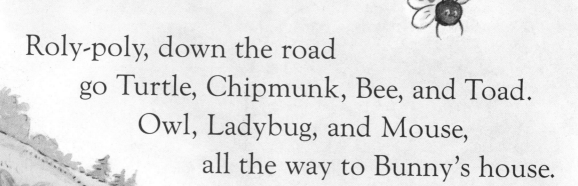

Roly-poly, down the road
　　go Turtle, Chipmunk, Bee, and Toad.
　　Owl, Ladybug, and Mouse,
　　　　all the way to Bunny's house.

Yoo-hoo, Bunny!
Dry your eyes.
Guess who's brought
a big surprise?

Hip-hop-hippity-hay
HOORAY!

Bunny's friends have saved the day.

Hippity, yippity, job well done.
HAPPY EASTER, everyone!